CHAPTER
1

"Let's go outside!" Turtle says.

Part of me wants to. Part of me does not. We've already been out to play in the snow twice today, and my snow pants and jacket are soaked.

"Come on, Twig," Turtle coaxes. "I'm tired of inside." She's been creating cotton-ball kittens with little pink ears and googly eyes while I've been reading.

I'm tired of being inside too. It's school vacation week. It snowed Saturday and Sunday and Monday

(which meant we canceled our visit to Grandma's). Now it's Tuesday, and we've been playing the same games, reading the same books, and crafting with the same supplies for three days. And the snow is still coming down!

"I've got cabin fever," Mom says as she plays with her camera.

"You mean *tiny-house* fever," Turtle says.

At first, the snow was really fun. It covered our skylights and drifted partway up the windows,

Time for Teamwork

READ MORE ADVENTURES ABOUT TWIG AND TURTLE!

1: Big Move to a Tiny House

2: Toy Store Trouble

3: Quiet Please!

4: Make New Friends, But Keep the Old

TWIG AND TURTLE

Time for Teamwork

Jennifer Richard Jacobson

Illustrated by Paula Franco

PIXEL✚INK

For Dad with love

PIXEL✚INK

Text copyright © 2021 by Jennifer Richard Jacobson
Illustrations copyright © 2021 by TGM Development Corp.
All rights reserved
Pixel+Ink is a division of TGM Development Corp.
Printed and bound in August 2021 at Maple Press, York, PA, U.S.A.
Cover and interior design by Georgia Morrissey
www.pixelandinkbooks.com
Library of Congress Control Number: 2021930050
Hardcover ISBN 978-1-64595-077-6
Paperback ISBN 978-1-64595-078-3
eBook ISBN 978-1-64595-079-0
First Edition
1 3 5 7 9 10 8 6 4 2

making our tiny house feel like a snow fort.

But even playing in a snow fort can get old.

I know because we built one in the backyard yesterday.

I retrieve my snow pants and parka, which are hanging in the shower. They're practically dripping. "Ugh!" I say. "These are still soaked."

Mom looks up from her camera. "Why don't you take them next door to Sudsy's and pop them in the dryer?" she suggests.

Yes! My snow clothes will come out toasty warm, and I'll get to say hi to Dad, who's working in

Sudsy's back room. Dad creates comic books. Mom is a photographer. Mr. Bryant, the owner of Sudsy's Laundromat, lets my parents use his back room for their studio. (*Studio* is an artsy name for *office*.)

"I don't care if my clothes are wet," Turtle says. "I have a shiny new idea, and I want to get started."

"What's your *shiny* idea?" I ask. In addition to the snow fort, we've already made snow angels, a snow family, and a small slide on top of a giant snowdrift.

"You'll see," she says, pulling up her snow-pants straps.

"Okay, but I'm drying my snow clothes first." I slip on my boots, but I don't even bother putting on my jacket. Sudsy's is practically a hop away—and besides, the mountain air feels cool and refreshing after being inside for the past couple hours.

Mr. Bryant is taking a load of clothes out of the

washer as I walk in. Sometimes, people sit on the benches and wait for their clothes to wash and dry. Sometimes, they pop in and out of the laundromat, doing errands in town while the machines do their work. And sometimes, customers drop off their clothes with Mr. Bryant, and he does the washing, drying, and folding for them.

From the looks of it today, Mr. Bryant has been left with a mountain of laundry.

"Many families have lost power this week," he explains to me.

Fortunately, there's still a free dryer.

You need a special card to make the Sudsy's machines run. I go into the studio to retrieve ours.

"Hey, Dad!" I say, peeking over his shoulder.

He looks up.
"Twigster! What are you up to?"

It looks like Dad's creating a new character. A pika! I didn't even

know what a pika was until we moved to Colorado. If you ask me, they look like giant mice and are pretty cute. And the one Dad is drawing has the funniest face.

"I need to dry my snow clothes," I explain. "Then Turtle and I are going to play outside. She has a *shiny* idea she won't share with me yet."

Dad laughs. "That girl always has shiny ideas!" He takes our laundry card off the shelf and hands it to me.

I smile. It's true. Turtle does have a lot of ideas. And most of them are unexpected. I can't help wondering: *Do I have shiny ideas too?*

I think of asking my dad, but it's his sacred time to get work done.

"Hey!" he says as I go back into the main room. "Let me know when you're heading back outside. I may be ready for a break."

"Will do," I tell him.

I place my wet clothes in the dryer and watch them tumble around behind the glass window for a few moments. The *thump, thump, thump* is soothing.

Mr. Bryant stands at the window. "Look at that snow come down," he says.

"Snowman flakes," I reply. Grandma taught me that snowflakes that look like the kind you cut from

paper are the best for rolling and packing into big snowballs. "They'll stick together."

"And cover my walk again," says Mr. Bryant with a sigh. He begins folding a mound of cloth diapers.

"Can I help?" I ask. "I'm a good folder, and it will give me something to do while I wait."

"Absolutely!" Mr. Bryant says. He steps away from the pile. "Have at it!"

I finish folding just as the dryer with my clothes beeps. At first, my snow pants are almost too hot to touch. But not for long. I slip them on and feel the warmth seep through my jeans.

I pop my head into the studio. "Heading outside, Dad!"

He slides his chair away from the desk and grabs his parka. "Break time!"

Mr. Bryant grabs his coat too. "I'll follow you," he

says. "I want to see if the sidewalk cleanup crew is making its way toward Sudsy's yet."

Mr. Bryant's walkway hasn't been shoveled in a while, but that's not what we notice. A small crowd has gathered in the space between our tiny house and Sudsy's. It doesn't take me long to figure out why.

Turtle has carved herself a little table and chair within the snowbank. And beside them, she's posted a sign.

Kids, teens, parents, and even one grandad want to buy cute cotton-ball snow kittens from Turtle.

Mom steps out to see what all the commotion is.

Dad joins Mom on the porch. You can tell they are both a little amazed by Turtle. They smile at me and shake their heads.

Mrs. Wallaby, the toy store owner, stops to see

what Turtle is up to. "Your daughter sure is enterprising!" she says.

I'm not sure what *enterprising* means. But it sounds good. Creative. Special.

Suddenly, I wish it was me sitting in that little snow chair.

I wish I was enterprising.

CHAPTER 2

Mr. Bryant trudges over the snow that's accumulated in front of his door. "Thanks for folding the diapers," he calls to me. "You were a big help."

"You're welcome!" I say. I may not be *enterprising*, but knowing I was helpful makes me feel good. *Hey!* I think. *I know another way I can be helpful.*

I race over to Cara's food truck, which sits on the other side of our tiny house.

"Hello, Miss Twig!" Cara says as I approach her

window. "Are you here for your favorite carrot muffins?" The name of Cara's food truck is Cara's Carrots and everything she cooks is made from carrots.

"Hmm. Not really," I say. "I was wondering if I could borrow your shovel?" I know Cara has one, because Mom and Dad forgot to pack one when we moved to Happy Trails, and they've been borrowing Cara's to shovel a path from the sidewalk to our porch.

"Of course!" she says. "It's in the shed out back."

I turn to go fetch the shovel, but she calls me back. "Taste this for me, love," Cara says as she reaches out with a cookie.

I pull my mitten off and happily take a bite. "Yum! It's delicious!

"Does it have enough nutmeg?"

I nod. Lots of carrot goodies have nutmeg. It's one of my favorite spices. (If I had a pet pika, I'd name it Nutmeg.)

I thank Cara for the cookie and head out back for the shovel.

Cara's shed is a mess! There are rakes and strings of lights, plant pots, and some shiny equipment I don't even recognize—which must be for cooking.

Fortunately, the shovel is easy to spot. It's bright orange (like a carrot!), and it's still snowy from the last use.

I grab it, shut the door, and race back to Sudsy's.

As soon as I've plunged the shovel into a mound of snow, Mr. Bryant opens the door.

"Twig! What are you doing?"

"I'm shoveling—"

"I can see that you're shoveling. But this is too big a job for an eight-year-old. Thank you for retrieving a shovel. I'll get my coat."

"No! Let me try. I'm strong!" I say, even though I've never shoveled snow before.

"But as you pointed out yourself, this snow is wet, packing snow. It will be heavy."

"I can do it!"

Here's what someone looks like when they want

to say no, but don't want to hurt your feelings:

- Their mouth smiles, but their eyes do not.

- They hold their chin as if it were heavy.

- Their shoulders droop.

"Okay," he says with a sigh. "But when you get tired, tell me. We can swap jobs. I'll shovel, and you can fold."

I nod. But I am determined to do this!

It isn't easy. I find I can't fill the snow shovel. When I do, it's too heavy for me to lift. So I only fill it partway. It will take me longer, but I think I can create a path from the sidewalk to the door.

Whoo! My arms start to feel tired, so I decide to take a rest. When I look through Sudsy's windows, Mr. Bryant is standing there. He points at himself as if to say, *My turn?*

I shake my head and get back to work. I really

want to complete this job.

I get so hot shoveling, I take off my coat and toss it on the snowbank I'm creating. Then I stand back and look at my path. It's wide in some areas and too skinny in others, so I work to make it wider in those spots.

I'm just about finished, when a woman with a toddler arrives at Sudsy's. I recognize her! Turtle

gave her a tour of our tiny house once. I step out of the path to let her through.

"Did you shovel this walkway?" she asks.

I nod. I'm pretty proud of the work I've done.

Mr. Bryant opens the door. "Can you believe an eight-year-old made this path, Mrs. Jones?"

"Well done!" Mrs. Jones says.

I leave the shovel next to the door and head back into the laundromat to get Dad. I want him to see my walkway too. But Mr. Bryant waves me over to the folding table where he and Mrs. Jones are standing.

"And she folded your baby's diapers!" Mr. Bryant adds.

"My word!" she says. "I may have to hire you myself!"

"Quite right!" Mr. Bryant goes to his cash register and takes out a five-dollar bill. "Here you go, Twig!"

he says as he holds it out to me.

I hesitate for a moment. I didn't mean for him to pay me. I was just trying to be helpful.

"You earned it!" Mr. Bryant says, and puts the bill in my hand.

"Well, look at that!" Dad says, poking his head out of the office. "Both you and your sister earned some money today. Maybe you can take Mom and me out to dinner tonight!"

I laugh. Dad's a real kidder.

Turtle has always liked saving money more than I have, but I'll admit, it feels fun to have money in my pocket.

Perhaps today I've been enterprising too!

CHAPTER 3

Before going to bed, I sit on the couch and use Dad's tablet to look up the word *enterprising*. It seems like it means *imaginative*, but in a taking-charge sort of way.

No doubt about it, Turtle definitely knows how to take charge. On her first day of school at Happy Trails Elementary, she taught her classmates a game called Follow My Directions.

"I made six dollars today!" Turtle says as I crawl into my sleeping bag next to her.

I find my favorite bed toys, Flat Bear and Snow Puff, and snuggle in for a good night's sleep. I could say, *And I made five dollars shoveling Mr. Bryant's walk*, but I don't. Turtle knows. She's just naming all the good things that happened to her during the day. It's her way of settling down to sleep.

"And Jordan and I made a plan to meet in the park tomorrow," she says, her voice growing a little fainter.

Sometimes, I list the good things that happened to me along with her, but tonight I prefer to remember them in my mind.

I start to remind Turtle that we completed the three-hundred-piece fish puzzle in record time— that was a good thing. (When you live in a tiny house, you can't have lots of puzzles, so we do the same one over and over and time ourselves to see how fast we can complete it.) But I can tell by her breathing she's already drifting off.

So instead, I look up at the stars through the skylight and think my own thoughts. I'm proud of the jobs I did for Mr. Bryant today. *That was taking charge in a good way*, I think. I acted before anyone suggested I fold diapers or shovel snow.

I liked seeing that neat stack of diapers and that cleared walkway. It makes me want to do other jobs for people. Like maybe organize Cara's shed.

The next morning, we have a video call with Grandma. It's Turtle's turn to talk first. "Look at this snow kitten I made!" she says.

"I definitely have to have one of those!" Grandma tells her. "Your mom sent me a picture of your snow shop! It sounds like you made lots of money."

"I did!" Turtle says. "And I'm going to give some of it to the local food pantry so everyone can have food in their cupboards."

What? Where have I heard those words before?

Then I remember. That's what the donation jar on the counter of Cara's food truck says: "Give so everyone has food in the cupboard."

I didn't know Turtle was going to donate her money. I wish I'd thought of that first.

Finally, it's my turn to talk. I tell Grandma about the snow fort Turtle and I made—how it's big enough for both of us to curl up inside. Then I tell her about shoveling Mr. Bryant's walkway.

"That's so kind of you!" Grandma says, and I get a glow-y feeling again. "I wish I had a handy person like you nearby. I could use some help around the apartment."

And that's when my own enterprising idea is born.

❧

"I'm going to start my own business," I say to
Mom when we get off the video call.

"You are?" She's taking pictures of the ice on our
window, so I can't tell if she's really paying attention.

"You're copying," Turtle says, folding her arms.

"No, I'm not," I tell her as I retrieve my snow
clothes from the bathroom again. The snow is
coming down lightly now, so we're heading to the
park. I'm hoping my best buds, Angela and David,
will be there—and our other friends too!

"Yes, you are," Turtle says. "You're copying
Turtle's Snow Kitten Shop." She grabs her snow
pants and starts wiggling inside them.

"I'm not!" I insist. "I'm not going to have a shop.
I'm going to have a handy-girl business."

27

Turtle looks at me with big eyes. "I want one of those businesses too!"

"*Now* who's copying?" I reply. "Besides, you probably don't even know what I'm talking about."

"If I don't know what you're talking about, how

can I copy?" Turtle asks.

"Who's ready for the park?" Dad says in a voice that also means *Stop. Your. Squabbling.*

I know I'm ready for the park. I'm ready for outside and playing with friends.

But I'm also looking forward to the walk. 'Cause I'm going to think about my new business every step of the way.

CHAPTER 4

The snow has stopped, and the streets of Happy Trails look like a fairyland covered in glistening white. The air is cold but smells clean and piney.

"It looks like the sky is clearing," I say.

"Maybe we can visit Grandma tomorrow!" Turtle says.

"Unfortunately not," says Mom. "Grandma has a busy schedule."

One of the expressions Grandma uses all the time is "I am of two minds." And that's exactly how I feel now. One of my minds is disappointed that I can't see my grandmother.

The other mind is happy to have a whole day tomorrow to make a flyer for my new business—complete with pictures! I think of the jobs I can list: folding clothes, shoveling snow, cleaning sheds, and . . . and walking dogs!

I have lots of practice in dog walking. We take care of Bo, the school reading dog, a lot. He used to live with my grandmother, but now he lives with Mr. Kim, the school custodian.

I'm imagining printing my flyers and handing them out to people, when I hear my name called.

"Twig!"

It's Matteo coming down the sidewalk in the opposite direction. He's in my class and he's one of my soccer buddies. Matteo is carrying a red plastic saucer and climbing over snow drifts still piled up in front of the park entrance.

"Hi, Matteo!" I call out.

"Twig!" he shouts again. "We're going sledding! Are you in?"

"Sledding!" Dad says. "Of course!"

"I bet they use the big hill that runs behind the duck pond," Mom says.

We're still figuring things out here in Happy Trails.

Turtle speeds up. "I hope Jordan has something to slide on!"

But Dad's hardly listening. Sometimes he's a bigger kid than we are. "I'll run back and see if Mrs. Wallaby has a couple snow tubes!" he says.

"But where will we keep them?" Mom asks. When you live in a tiny house, that question gets asked all the time.

"They deflate!" Dad replies. "We can keep them in the storage closet in the studio."

Mom's forehead wrinkles. "That storage closet is getting mighty full."

But Dad isn't listening. He's racing back to the toy store. Mom notices Matteo's mother coming up the sidewalk with Matteo's brother in a back carrier. She waits to chat with her.

I run to catch up with Matteo. I'm hoping he'll share his saucer with me until Dad gets back.

The park in winter looks entirely different. Piled snow has turned all of the playground equipment into snow creatures. But there are well-worn paths, made from stomping boots, through the creatures and up to the top of the sledding hill. I feel a chill and I'm not sure if it's because of the cold or the excitement of sledding.

My wish comes true. It seems as if my entire class is at the park. I spot Angela and David and Effie by the big oak at the top of the hill. Matteo follows me.

"Don't you have a sled?" David asks. He looks concerned.

Everyone has something to slide with except me. "My dad went to Mrs. Wallaby's to see if he can buy some," I say.

"You can share with me!" Angela calls.

"And we can all hold hands as we go down the hill," Effie adds. "Like one big train!"

Like Turtle, Effie has lots of creative ideas.

So we line up. Effie has a snow tube. She's in the front. She reaches back for David's hand.

David has a long plastic sled. He lies down on his tummy.

Angela can't take David's hand, so she holds onto his boot.

I'm behind Angela. I turn around backward so I can hold onto Matteo's saucer. He's bringing up the rear.

I hear Turtle's laugh. I turn and I see her on the front of Jordan's sled, flying down the hill. Snow sprays in all directions.

"Ready?" Effie asks.

I tighten my grip on Matteo's saucer . . . and we're off!

It doesn't take long for our train to break apart.
Effie flips. David lets go to avoid a crash. When
he does, his boot comes off in Angela's hand.

I'm afraid Matteo is going to fly right into us, so I let go and he goes spinning off, barely avoiding some other kids on tubes.

Angela and I end up in a heap at the bottom of the hill. We can't stop laughing. David hops over to

us on one foot to retrieve his boot. Matteo and Effie plop down beside us.

"Now let's have a race!" Angela says.

"Yeah!" says Matteo.

"You can ride with me this time," David tells me.

We trudge back up the hill. I look around to see if my dad has returned from the toy store. Mom is talking with some of her friends by the oak tree, but I can't spot Dad.

David places the sled at the start line. "You be in front."

"I'm not sure I'm good at steering," I say.

"No one is good at steering this kind of sled. If it looks like we're going to hit something—or someone—yell '*NOW!*' and we'll roll off."

My friends and I get into race position. Angela yells, "One, two, three, GO!"

And we're flying down the hill. The cold air slaps my face and nearly takes my breath away. I try to keep my eyes open and lean away from other sledders.

Suddenly, I see a bump up ahead.

WOMP! We're airborne for a moment and then we land—turned around.

We reach the bottom of the hill backward. None of my friends fall off this time.

"Great ride!" David calls.

Matteo starts piling the snow into columns beside us. "Look! I'm making snow pins—like bowling pins. Let's see how many we can knock down on our next run."

Another great idea! We help him make a whole bunch of pins, hoping no one will knock them down before we get to the top of the hill.

Fortunately, most kids think they're meant to be a sculpture (like weird snow zombies), so they're all still standing when we reach the top and get into position.

"Ready . . . GO!" Matteo yells, and we bump and slide toward the pins. This time, I'm sitting between Effie's legs on her snow tube. We go so fast! We fly over the tops of the pins, only shaving one.

But the other kids crash into them.

I try to think of the next fun thing to do. Here are my ideas:

- Sledding backward? (Too many people.)
- Play follow-the-leader? (Too many of us to keep on course.)
- Play bumper sleds? (Too dangerous.)

But I do have an idea I'm dying to share. So while we're all lying in the snow—and David eats a handful and says it tastes like ginger ale, and we all give it a try (it doesn't)—I tell them about my idea to start my own business.

"That's so cool!" says Angela.

"We can help!" says David.

"I'm really good at vacuuming!" Matteo says.

"And I can decorate people's bathrooms!" Effie says.

I'm not exactly sure people want their bathrooms

decorated. I'm trying to think of a way to say this gently, but all my friends are building on my idea.

Angela: "We can wash windows!"

Matteo: "Cars!"

David: "We can paint rooms!"

Angela: "What can we buy with the money?"

Matteo: "A four-wheeler!"

It feels like my business is getting away from me—that it's no longer mine.

Effie: "We can have a vote—"

"Wait!" I say, a little louder than I planned.

My friends go quiet.

"This is MY handy-girl business," I say.

More quiet.

"At least at first," I add to be kinder.

"Oh," Angela finally says.

"By yourself?" asks David.

I want to say, *Yes, I want to try it on my own.*

But I don't get the chance.

Because in the next moment, we hear "Cowabunga!"

We all whip around on cue.

It's Dad!

In a snow tube!

Barreling right toward us!

CHAPTER
5

The next day, I start my project right after breakfast. Dad opens a program on his laptop that's useful for creating things like flyers. He shows me how to drag photos into the document and how to create boxes for writing.

Once I type the information, he tells me I can change the colors and the look of the letters.

"You mean the *font*?" I ask.

He nods, remembering that I've had practice making projects like birthday cards before.

I start to list all the odd jobs I might be able to
do, but it seems too willy-nilly. Washing windows
comes after training your dog to sit . . . which comes
after sorting your junk drawer. So I organize the
things I can do into three columns:

Cleaning	Organizing	Helper
Windows	Sheds	Doing laundry
Vacuuming	Drawers	Watching baby
Dusting	Tupperware	Dog walking
Pots and pans	Toy shelves	Delivering food

Dad looks at my work. "You might want to pick a font that's easier to read," he says.

I stare at it. I like my font. I think it shows creativity. I just shrug.

"It's *your* flyer," he says, walking away.

Next, I look for photos to add. My teacher, Mr. Harbor, showed us how to find free photos that don't require permission to use. I choose a picture of a girl folding her own laundry and drop it into my flyer. I also select a photo of another girl walking a Great Dane that looks just like Bo!

Mom looks over my shoulder. "You could crop that picture," she suggests. "Then you'd be able to see the face of the dog walker."

"I know," I say, but I really don't think it matters, so I keep it as it is.

Once I finish my flyer and get dressed, I head

47

over to our studio to print it.

Dad comes too. "Make only the number of copies you need to—"

"To save ink and trees," I say, finishing his sentence for him.

Here are the people I decide to print a flyer for:

• Mr. Bryant, owner of Sudsy's

• Cara, chef and owner of Cara's Carrots

• Mrs. Wallaby, owner of Mrs. Wallaby's Toy Store

• Mr. Kim, dog-parent to Bo

• Mrs. Jones, mother of a toddler named Wendy

I wonder if I should make one for my parents, but I know that they'll say doing chores is being part of a family, so I don't bother.

As soon as the first flyer is printed, I rush out to show Mr. Bryant.

"What a smart idea!" he says. "How much do you charge for these jobs?"

Oh.

Prices.

I should have included prices.

I think for a minute. Some jobs, like dusting, are fairly easy. And some jobs, like shoveling, are harder. But I'll never remember the prices if I make them all different. Should I run back and stop the printer?

Nah, I want to start handing these out. "Every job is two dollars," I say. That should make keeping track of payment easy.

TWIG'S
HANDY GIRL BUSINESS

"Very reasonable," he says. Then he nods. "Some people in Happy Trails still don't have power. It will be busy here today. I'll have you do some folding for me."

Yay! I got my very first job—and I did it all by myself!

"I'd love to," I tell him.

"Great," he says. "Why don't you come back after lunch?"

Perfect. That will give me time to hand out my flyers.

I'm going to be a handy girl!

CHAPTER 6

I stop briefly at home to tell Mom that I'm leaving to hand out my flyers.

"Let me help!" Turtle says, reaching for her coat.

"No, this is *my* business," I reply, but it comes out meaner than I mean it to.

"Please?"

"You were going to make more snow kittens to sell," I remind her.

Turtle's shoulders fall, but then her face brightens. "I do want to open my snow shop this afternoon."

Phew.

Mom comes over to the door and zips my parka up to my chin. "Be careful," she says. "The sidewalks will be slippery."

"I may not be back right away," I tell her. "People might want to hire me on the spot."

She smiles. "I've raised two businesswomen," she says, before pulling Turtle and me in for a hug.

"Just like you, Mom," Turtle replies.

I tell Mom that I'll be visiting Cara and Mrs. Wallaby (I'm not sure where Mrs. Jones lives), and then head over to Cara's Carrots.

"What can I get you, Miss Twig?" Cara asks as I carefully approach her window.

"This time, I have something for you!" I say, reaching up with a flyer.

"Oh, can I use you!" she says, glancing at my lists.

"Each job costs two dollars!" I tell her.

"Very reasonable!" she says, just like Mr. Bryant did. (I probably should charge three dollars for each job—or even five dollars, like Mr. Bryant paid me yesterday.)

"I'd love for you to wash pots and pans. I've got a stack already!"

"And how about organizing your shed?" I ask.

"Yes, please!" she says, opening the door on her food truck so I can step inside. "But why don't you start with these pots and see how you feel afterward?"

I can tell she's underestimating me the same way that Mr. Bryant did. "You'll see," I say, reaching for one of her aprons, which hangs on a hook. "I'm a hard worker."

"I don't doubt that for a moment," she says, but for some reason I think she might.

Here's how you know when an adult is saying one thing, but thinking more:

- There's a twinkle in their eye (like there's a joke you might not have heard).
- They turn away quickly so "the more" won't discourage you or hurt your feelings.

I reach for a bowl with lots of carrot-something batter stuck to the sides, then fill it with hot soapy water.

Cara hands me her extra-stiff scrubbing brush, and I put all my arm strength into getting the stuck-on layers off.

When I have one clean bowl, I empty the yucky water, dry the bowl, and place it back on Cara's shelf. Then I reach for a greasy frying pan and do the same thing.

Because Cara is cooking as I'm washing, I never

run out of pans: muffin tins, cake pans, soup pots. Even the first bowl with the stuck-on batter comes around again. This time, it's filled with pieces of shredded carrot. I wonder how Cara manages to clean up after herself every single day.

Dad stops by to see if I want to come home for lunch, but I'm already munching on carrot potpie.

By the time I finish eating, Cara's too busy selling her yummy goodies to dirty up any more dishes.

"Why don't you come by tomorrow?" she says, handing me four dollars instead of two! "We can get started on that very messy shed."

"Thank you!" I say. "I'll be here!"

Even though I told Mr. Bryant that I'd come by after lunch, I'm eager to visit Mrs. Wallaby and give her my flyer. If I hurry, I'll have time to do both.

As I head in the direction of the toy store, the sun is shining brightly, and I'm surprised by how much ice has melted on the sidewalks. Water drips from tree limbs and rooftops. A stream of water runs down the back of my neck as I pass under the awning at Tres Café, Mom's favorite coffee shop. I hardly notice it.

Hey! I wonder if they need any extra help at Tres Café. And what about Georgia at the Vintage Store? Maybe she could use some help organizing? *I'll have*

56

to print off some more flyers, I think.

When I pop into Mrs. Wallaby's Toy Store, I suddenly begin to imagine all the things I'll be able to buy with the money I'm earning. (That is, whatever can fit on my toy shelf. As Mom and Dad say, "Tiny spaces, big limits.")

I'm considering a songwriting kit, a Universe Doll, and a snow-cone machine (maybe it could be for the family and stored in the kitchen?) when Mrs.Wallaby comes out from her back room.

"Hi, Twig!" she says. "What can I do for you?"

"Um . . . oh!" (For a moment, I forgot. I was so busy imagining my future shopping spree!)

"I actually came in to see if there's something I can do for you!" I say as I hand her one of my flyers.

"What's this?" she asks, adjusting her glasses and reading slowly.

I want to say, *I could dust your shelves*, but I don't want her to think I'm suggesting her shelves are dirty.

"I see something I can use," she says finally. "Tomorrow, Mrs. Jones comes in to help me with my accounting."

"Mrs. Jones who has that cute baby, Wendy?"

"That's right," Mrs. Wallaby says. "I think we might get more done if you were here to watch her."

Yes! I can't believe my luck! I'll get to watch Wendy, check out the toys, and hand Mrs. Jones a flyer!

"Can you be here at ten a.m.?" Mrs. Wallaby asks.

"Absolutely!" I tell her. That will give me time to clean up Cara's shed before I need to be back at the toy store.

I can't wait to get home to tell Mom and Dad how

enterprising I am!

That is, I think, *after I help Mr. Bryant with his folding.*

CHAPTER 7

The next morning, I sleep later than I'd planned to. I guess doing odd jobs is more tiring than I thought it would be.

While I was folding laundry yesterday, Mr. Bryant asked if I could come back this morning to do some more. I promised I would—before cleaning Cara's shed and babysitting for Wendy.

But when I pop out the door on the way to Sudsy's, David and Angela greet me on my front porch.

"We're at the park," Angela says. "We got permission to come and get you. Do you want to build a snow rocket under the slide with us?"

"A snow rocket sounds like fun, but I can't," I tell them, before pulling my handy-girl flyer out of my pocket and holding it out for them to see. "I have some jobs to do today."

"Wow! Your flyer looks so cool!" Angela says.

"You made this?" asks David. "It's awesome."

"Yesterday I washed Cara's pots and pans and folded laundry for Mr. Bryant. Today I'm—"

"You got to go inside Cara's food truck?" David interrupts, his eyes wide.

I nod. "And today I'm folding more laundry, cleaning a shed, and watching a baby!"

I hope I don't sound like I'm bragging.

"Are you sure you don't want help?" Angela asks.

"We could work with you after we build the rocket."

"And the remote-control panel," says David. "Don't forget that."

Angela nods. "And the secret passageway to get into the rocket."

"Thanks anyway," I say. "But I've got this."

Fortunately, David and Angela don't seem to mind. They're eager to get back to the park.

For a moment, I think of joining them. Creating a secret tunnel that leads inside a rocket sounds

supercool. Maybe I could play until I have to babysit, and then clean the shed and fold laundry?

No. Mr. Bryant is expecting me, and I'm already late.

"Maybe I can help with the rocket this afternoon," I call out to my friends as they head back to the park. But neither seem to hear me.

Oh, well. I jog into the laundromat and get a second surprise.

Bo is here! With Mr. Kim!

I wrap my arms around Bo's neck.

"I hear you're doing odd jobs," Mr. Kim says.

I nod and pull the flyer from my pocket. "I thought you might like me to give Bo some extra walks!" I tell him.

Mr. Kim looks at my flyer and smiles. "I made a list of odd jobs just like this one when I was your age!"

"You did?" I like knowing that.

"Yes, my brother and I did it together. One woman asked me if I knew how to iron clothes. 'Of course, I do!' I told her, but I had never ironed in my life. I made a big black burn mark right in the middle of her blouse."

I bite my bottom lip and decide right then and there that I will not tell anyone that I can iron. (I've never seen anyone I know iron, so that should be easy.)

"I'd like to hire you, Twig," he says. "Not for dog walking, but for a few hours of dog watching. How about today?"

"Today?" I have to think for a moment. I've already made promises to Mr. Bryant, Cara, and Mrs. Wallaby.

"If you watch Bo, I can visit my mother," Mr. Kim explains. "Her apartment building doesn't allow dogs."

Hmm. Mr. Bryant allows dogs in Sudsy's, and Bo can be outside while I clean out Cara's shed. I'm not sure about Mrs. Wallaby's, but maybe I can leave Bo at our house while I'm taking care of Wendy. . . .

"Yes!" I say. "I'd be happy to."

"Great," says Mr. Kim, grabbing his basket of

laundry. "I'll pick Bo up at your house this afternoon. Say about three o'clock?"

Bo and I wave goodbye to Mr. Kim, then we join Mr. Bryant at the folding table. He slides some kids' clothes my way. I fold lots of little jeans and printed shirts. One shirt has a moose on it. Another has cacti and the words PLANET PROTECTOR.

"I'm way behind," says Mr. Bryant. "I may have you do some laundry for me today in addition to folding. Would you like that? You know how to operate the washers and dryers, don't you?"

I do! Our parents do all of our laundry here at Sudsy's, so I've had plenty of practice. I don't think cleaning Cara's shed will take long, and I doubt Wendy's mother plans to be at the toy store for very long either. I haven't done any official babysitting, but from what I can tell, babies need lots of changes in scenery.

67

"I'd love to do laundry!" I tell Mr. Bryant. "But I promised Cara and Mrs. Wallaby that I'd do jobs for them today too. Would it be okay if I fold now and do laundry after lunch?"

"You are a wonder!" Mr. Bryant replies. "Let's make sure that it's all right with your parents. And you can change your mind if you decide you've done enough jobs for one day."

"Okay."

Mr. Bryant and I finish folding the laundry and place it in a bag. He shows me the basket of dirty clothes behind the desk that will need washing later. "Great!" I say. "You can count on me!"

Bo, who has been lying at my feet, sits up and licks my hand as if to say, *Come on. What's next?* Dogs like changes in scenery too.

I stop by my house to ask my parents for

permission to do laundry later, but I quickly see they're in a virtual meeting. Mom gives me big eyes that tell me that Bo, who she hadn't planned on seeing today, is not welcome at this moment. So I pantomime heading over to Cara's to help clean her shed. I'm not sure my mom understood, but she seemed happy for me to leave.

Cara gives me the key to her shed, and as soon as I open the door, I remember why she needs me. There's so much stuff tangled together! I decide that the best way to organize the shed is to pull everything out. Then I'll group things together and put them back in place.

I pull out plant pots, rakes, paintbrushes, lime green lawn chairs, a red wagon, and a big cooking pot.

I'm getting so hot carrying things, I unzip my parka.

For a while, Bo follows me in and out of the shed, but then he finds a ball. He throws it up in the air, then digs in the snow to find it again. This keeps him happy.

There's so much stuff, I have to place some of it in front of the food truck. Fortunately, Cara doesn't

seem to mind. She gives me a thumbs-up and goes back to cooking.

I'm trying to untangle a string of lights when I hear a man, who is standing in line at Cara's, tell his son that it's almost ten! I'm supposed to be watching Wendy in four minutes! Yikes!

"I'll be back soon!" I call to Cara.

I pop my head into my house, but I don't see Turtle or my parents. (Where did they go?) I can't leave Bo alone. The last time Bo was alone in our house, he stood up on his hind feet and pulled everything off the shelves.

"Come on, Bo!" I call. "I've got to get to Mrs. Wallaby's Toy Store, and you're coming with me."

CHAPTER
8

The day has gotten warmer, and I'm feeling hot as we race together down the slushy sidewalk. Twice, I slide and almost fall on my bum!

We arrive, and I quickly tie Bo to a bench outside the store and rush inside. The bell over the door announces my arrival.

"Here she is," says Mrs. Wallaby with her eyeglasses halfway down her nose. I can tell that she's not too happy with my lateness.

"Sorry, I'm late," I say. "Hi, Wendy!"

Wendy smiles and reaches her arms out to me, just like she did the first time I met her.

I take her, careful to hold her tightly. She smells like Play-Doh and mushy Cheerios.

"We'll be right out back," Mrs. Jones says. "Come and get me if you need me."

I tell her I will, and then Wendy kicks her legs, letting me know that she's had enough holding. She's eager to get down. I gently lower her onto the floor, and she immediately crawls off.

"Oh," says Mrs. Wallaby, pointing to a bag near the cash register. "Those are Wendy's toys in there."

I nod, knowing that she's also saying, *Don't play with the toys for sale.*

I pull a few toys out of the bag and present them to Wendy. But she's totally uninterested in them.

This baby wants to move! She's a speedy crawler with a whole store to cover.

Fortunately, it doesn't take long to find a game she loves. Here are the instructions:

- Watch baby disappear down an aisle.

- Pop your head around the corner and say, "Boo!"

- Laugh along with baby.

- Do it again.

And again.

And again.

I glance out the window, trying to think of a new game as popular as Find Wendy, and notice a group of teenagers walking down the sidewalk in a straight line. The one in front is pulling a red wagon. I wonder what they're going to do with a wagon in the snow. The next kid is carrying an orange shovel— just like Cara's.

The third kid is wrapped in a string of lights. I feel like I'm watching a parade.

It *is* a parade. A parade of Cara's stuff! They're carrying the things I pulled out of the shed!

Could Cara have given all of that stuff to them? Even if she gave them the wagon and the lights, she probably wouldn't have given them her snow shovel.

Oh no.

It hits me.

In Happy Trails, people often put things in their

front yards for others to take—*for free*. It's an easy way to recycle the belongings you don't need anymore.

Did these kids think Cara's things were up for grabs?

I open the door and call out, but they don't hear me.

I watch them walking down the sidewalk . . . and if that's not bad enough, Bo frees himself in all the excitement and bounds after them. (I should have tied his leash tighter!)

Yikes! He can't be off on his own. Who knows what could happen?

"Bo!" I call. But wait—

Wendy!

I race to find her. She's in the back corner and has pulled a small wooden dollhouse from a bottom shelf down onto the floor. Thankfully, she's not hurt in any way that I can tell.

She sees me, laughs, and quickly crawls away.

As I go to put the dollhouse back onto the shelf, I see that it landed on a small canopy bed.

It's smashed to bits.

No!

Everything is going wrong.

I put the spilled furniture back in the dollhouse, and the dollhouse back on the shelf.

I feel like I can hardly breathe. Do I interrupt Mrs. Wallaby and tell her about the broken bed? (I can just picture her angry face.) Do I tell Mrs. Jones that I can't babysit any longer? That I have to find Bo before anything terrible happens to him?

These two confessions together would make me feel like a huge failure. (So long, Miss Enterprising.)

Then a new possibility occurs to me.

"Let's look out the door," I say, scooping Wendy up.

Bo loves kids and will follow them anywhere. I'm hoping the group notices that Bo is tracking them and they'll try to find his owner. That's what I would do.

Wendy slaps her hand against the glass.

So far, no sign of them.

But I do recognize someone else coming down the sidewalk from the opposite direction: Turtle!

I open the door and call out, "I'm so glad to see you!"

"You are?"

"Yes! What are you doing here?"

"Mom said you had Bo, and I wanted to see him. Then Mom remembered that you are watching Wendy, and she said I could come get Bo from you."

"Oh, Turtle, thank you. I'm so glad you're here. I need your help."

Turtle places her hands on her hips. "I thought you said you didn't—"

"I know. And I was so wrong. I need your help, and I need the help of my friends. I think they're at the park—by the slide. Will you go see if they're there? And if they are, will you ask them to come back with you?"

She makes a frowny face. "Mom said I could come here alone. She didn't say I could go to the *park* alone."

"Well, this is sort of an emergency. Besides, you won't be *staying* at the park. You'll only stop for a second to deliver a message. If the kids aren't there, come right back."

Turtle thinks for a moment, then nods. So I pop outside with Wendy and watch as Turtle makes her way. A drop of water falls off the arch above and runs down Wendy's face. She thinks it's hysterical.

I hope my friends are still at the park. They might have gone home by now, and then what?

My head is full of worries. Worries for Bo—anything could happen to him. And now worries for my little sister off by herself too.

What was I thinking?

Luckily, Mrs. Jones and Mrs. Wallaby finish their accounting. Mrs. Wallaby starts to pay me, but Mrs. Jones insists that *she's* the one who should pay me for looking after Wendy.

I know I need to tell Mrs. Wallaby what happened to the dollhouse bed, but I don't have time right now. I have to find my sister, locate sweet Bo, and get Cara's things back.

I accept the payment from Mrs. Jones, give Wendy a high five, and tell Mrs. Wallaby I'll be back soon.

Then I race to the park.

"Twig!" Turtle calls. She's by the park gate with the whole gang: Angela, David, Effie, and Matteo. They all have pink cheeks from playing outside.

I explain what happened. "We've got to find Bo! And when we do, we might just find the kids and Cara's things too."

"We could split up," Angela suggests.

"Good idea!" says David. "We could each take some side streets."

Matteo nods.

"Or we could just follow Bo's tracks in the snow," says Turtle.

Everyone stops talking and looks at her.

83

"Brilliant," Effie finally says.

It's so true. "You have the best ideas," I say to my little sister.

Together, we follow Bo's very big tracks.

Matteo cups his hands around his mouth and takes a big breath.

"Wait! Don't call Bo," Angela says. "If he hears

us call, he might leave the other kids, and then we won't be able to find them and get Cara's stuff."

She's right, but this is making me even more nervous.

What if Bo finds some other kids to follow? What if he gets into garbage and eats something he's not supposed to? What if he runs into traffic?

How could I have messed things up so badly?

CHAPTER 9

Bo's tracks lead us past the Vintage Store.

Past the post office.

Past a corner grocery store.

I'm worried that we're getting farther and farther from the park. I don't know about the other kids, but Turtle and I have never walked this far down Main Street by ourselves.

We reach Bud's Barbeque when Turtle shouts, "There he is!"

Sure enough, Bo is sitting in the snow next to a

picnic table where a group of teenagers is eating barbeque sandwiches.

And fortunately, it's the same group that took Cara's things.

My friends and I rush over and start talking all at once. Bo jumps up to greet me.

"Hold it," David shouts at us. Then he turns to the teenagers. "Twig can tell you everything."

So I do. I tell them how I was cleaning Cara's shed. How I had to stop and didn't have time to put all of her things away.

The teens are quiet for a moment. They look at one another as if wondering how to respond.

Finally, the girl with the snow shovel shrugs and says, "We were going to eat lunch at Cara's, but she had her Be Back in Five Minutes sign in the window." (I don't tell them Cara hops next door to

Sudsy's to use the bathroom there.)

"Yeah," says the boy who was pulling the wagon. "Then we started thinking this stuff was cool, and how we could use it one way or another. But you can have it back. We don't want you to get into trouble or anything."

"Wait a minute," says the boy wrapped in lights. "I really want these lights for my bedroom. Finders keepers."

"'Finders keepers' isn't a real law," says Matteo.

"Come on," says the girl. "Give them back."

"Cara probably doesn't even care," says the boy. "She's not using them, is she?"

Ack! This could go on forever!

I want to get back to the shed before any other things go missing. And I still have laundry to do! I place my hand in my pocket. "I have some money," I say. "I can buy the lights from you."

"How much?" the boy says.

The other two teenagers shout "No!" at the same time.

That's when the boy unwraps himself from the lights and hands them back to me.

"I'll tell Cara that you wanted them," I say. "Maybe she will be happy to let you have them."

The boy shrugs.

90

"Thanks!" I say to all three teens.

Angela grabs the wagon handle. Effie puts the lights around her neck. David grabs the shovel. Matteo grabs Bo's leash, and we start back.

We drop Matteo and Effie off at the park. Angela calls her mother on her phone and asks if she and David (her mom is watching David during vacation) can come with me to finish cleaning up Cara's shed. Her mom says yes!

As we approach the shed, I notice that the things I took out are spread all over the place. I wonder if Cara noticed the mess (how could she not?), or worse, that some of her things were missing. Either way, I hope she isn't mad. I'm going to have a lot of explaining to do when this day is over.

Turtle runs and gets a pencil and paper. She starts drawing a map of where different things should go inside the shed. (This is one of her superpowers.)

While Turtle is planning, the rest of us sweep and dust the shed.

Then we decide the different categories: small tools, large tools, kitchen items, things for summertime (umbrella, lawn chairs), things for wintertime (shovel, snowshoes). We put the summertime things, which won't be needed for a few more months, in the back.

I'm carrying plant pots (summertime thing) into the shed, when I hear a horn beep. It's Angela's mom here to pick up my friends.

Angela runs to talk to her mom and then races back. "Do you want to come to my house and play Universe Dolls?" she asks. "My mom says it's okay."

David gives a little hop. "Say yes!"

I glance around. There are still lots of things to return to Cara's shed. "I can't," I say to Angela and David, "but thanks anyway. And thanks for all your help! I'll share my earnings with you when I'm paid."

David nods. "Cool."

Angela smiles.

I watch them get in the car and wave when they drive away without me.

Then Turtle and I get back to work.

Because we're doing such a careful job, it takes a long time.

"Oh, my goodness!" I say suddenly. "It must be way past three, and I haven't done any laundry for Mr. Bryant yet."

"I can do it!" Turtle says. "I've done laundry with Mom and Dad lots of times."

I hesitate. It wasn't like I actually agreed to do laundry—I was supposed to ask Mom and Dad first. But I want to come through for Mr. Bryant and there's no way I can leave Cara's shed again.

"Okay," I say to Turtle. (Rats! I really wanted to

do it!) "Thanks for helping me even more. See if Mom or Dad will go with you."

Turtle nods. "Mom was going to work in the studio anyway."

I pop into our house and get Bo a big bowl of water and some treats.

Then I buckle down and put everything back into the shed as quickly as possible so I can help Turtle with the laundry.

I sigh as I drop the last armload in place.

Bo looks at me with one ear up and his head cocked to the side. *What's wrong, Twig?* he seems to say.

I take a big breath, bury my face in his neck, and

tell him all the ways I've messed up today.

There are so many.

Sharing my mistakes with Bo helps.

But only a little.

I want to show Cara her new-and-improved shed, but this is one of her busiest times. So instead, I head into Sudsy's. Turtle is doing the flamingo dance by one of the washing machines.

Bo wags his tail. He loves this dance.

"Where's Mr. Bryant?" I ask.

"He's gone to make some laundry deliveries. Mom is in the studio."

I am so proud of my sister. She figured out how to find Bo. She drew an awesome map for Cara's shed (which we hung on a nail inside). And now she's doing laundry for me and Mr. Bryant.

I'm about to tell her all of this when I stop and stare at the washer she loaded.

"Look, Turtle!" I exclaim.

Bubbles are escaping from the washing machine. They're tumbling over one another like a waterfall of suds!

"Maybe I didn't shut the washer right," Turtle says.

She opens the door and water and foam pour out.

Yikes!

CHAPTER 10

"Shut the door!" I yell.

Bo is slip-sliding in the water and suds all around us.

Turtle slams the door shut.

"This has never happened to me," I say. "What did you do?"

Turtle shrugs.

If there's anything I've learned today, it's this: Ask for help when you need it.

I race back into the studio, where Mom is looking at her photographs on the big computer screen.

"Mom!" I shout. "A washer is broken. Suds are everywhere!"

She gets up and races to the storage closet. "I'll get a mop and meet you out front," she says.

I peer through the washer window. You still can't see the clothes through the suds.

"Did you do anything differently today?" I ask Turtle, who has bubbles on her shoulders and in her hair.

"I couldn't find the laundry detergent," Turtle says.

"So what did you use?" I ask.

"I ran home and got the soap for washing dishes."

"That explains things," Mom says, coming up behind us with a mop and bucket. "Dishwashing soap makes loads more bubbles."

"What are we going to do?" I ask.

Mom shakes her head. "You mean, what are *you* going to do?" She hands me the mop. "After all, it's *your* handy-girl business."

"But Tur—"

I stop myself. Mom's right. It's my business, and

Turtle was only trying to help me. And if I've proven anything today, it's that everyone makes mistakes.

Mom goes back to the studio.

"I'm going to open my snow kitten shop for a while," Turtle says and heads out. (Sometimes I wish I were six again.)

I take the bucket and the mop and try to sop up the soap mess. It's much harder than it looks. There's a lot of mud on the floor, and it makes swirling patterns.

Bo watches.

When the washer stops, I try to pull out the clothes, but they're so full of soap, they're stiff and they cling together. I don't want to dry them like this.

So I wipe out as much of the suds from the washer as I can, and then restart the machine without using any soap this time.

When Mr. Kim arrives to pick up Bo, I notice that our Great Dane still has a sudsy beard.

"I can't thank you enough, Twig," Mr. Kim says to me. "I had a wonderful day with my mother."

"I'm sorry, Mr. Kim. I wasn't the best dog sitter," I tell him, brushing hair from my face. "At one point, Bo got away from me."

Mr. Kim raises his eyebrows.

"Next time, if I have to tie him for a moment, I'll tie him much tighter."

He nods. But I wonder if he'll trust me to watch Bo by myself again.

As I move the laundry from the washer to the dryer, I think about the past two days. There were happy times: folding with Mr. Bryant, playing ball with Bo, making Wendy laugh, sorting a shed with my sister and my friends. And there were problems:

being late, a broken toy, kids taking Cara's things, losing Bo, mopping. But I learned a lot.

Here are five things I now know about starting a successful business:

- Everything will take longer than you think it will.

- It is not smart to schedule too many things in a day.

- Ask for help when you need it.

- Mistakes will happen. (Apologize when they do.)

- Teamwork is the best.

Mr. Kim and Bo have just left when Cara pops into the laundromat.

"Miss Twig!" she says. "You are the best. My shed has never looked so good. Not even on the day I built it!"

Even though I'm apologizing, she just laughs when I tell her what happened to some of her things, and how Turtle and my friends helped me put the shed back together.

"Thank you for working so hard to make it right," she says. "Tell your friends to come see me," she says. "Free treats for all!"

"They'll love that!" I say.

Then she asks, "Would you be willing to work

for me again tomorrow? I have some cupboards I want you to sort. And more pots and pans for you to wash!"

I think for a moment. Tomorrow is going to be hard. I need to talk to Mrs. Wallaby and pay for the broken doll bed. (She is going to be so GROUCHY!) I need to talk to Mr. Bryant. And I need to catch up on my family chores.

"Thanks, Cara," I say, "but I can't tomorrow. I already have a full day. Would it be okay if I worked for you one day next week?"

"Sure," she says. "That would be great."

Great! Because as soon as I've met all my responsibilities, I really want to do one thing: Play in the snow with Turtle and my friends.

ABOUT THE AUTHOR

JENNIFER RICHARD JACOBSON is the award-winning author of many books for children and young adults, including the Andy Shane early-reader series and her most recent book, *Crashing in Love*. A graduate of Harvard Graduate School of Education, when not writing, Jennifer provides trainings in Writer's Workshop for teachers. Jennifer lives in Maine with her husband and dog.